THIS BOOK BELONGS TO

Rachel
Gbackizro

To Becky, Robin, Sibéal and Tia – RLO
For Rapha, my UBBFF – LB
To Emma – David O'Connell

Cover and interior illustrations by David O'Connell
Special thanks to Liz Bankes and Rebecca Lewis-Oakes

First published in Great Britain 2023 by Farshore

An imprint of HarperCollins*Publishers*
1 London Bridge Street, London SE1 9GF

farshore.co.uk

HarperCollins*Publishers*
Macken House, 39/40 Mayor Street Upper,
Dublin 1, D01 C9W8

Text copyright © 2023 Farshore
Illustrations copyright © 2023 David O'Connell

ISBN 978 0 00 850215 7
Printed and bound using 100% renewable electricity at CPI Group (UK) Ltd
1

A CIP catalogue record for this title is available from the British Library

THE NAUGHTIEST UNICORN

AND THE ICE DRAGON

PIP BIRD

ILLUSTRATED BY DAVID O'CONNELL

Contents

Chapter One: Neon-orange Snow Boots   1

Chapter Two: No Snow Festival   13

Chapter Three: The Wrong Crack   25

Chapter Four: Chilli-farts   37

Chapter Five: Chilly Fart-blasts   52

Chapter Six: Growing Pains   70

Chapter Seven: Good Egg   84

Chapter Eight: Let It Go   105

Chapter Nine: Bum Snow   117

Chapter Ten: Unicorn School Forever   132

CHAPTER ONE
Neon-orange Snow Boots

'This is going to be the best trip to Unicorn School EVER!' Mira jumped and punched the air in excitement.

'OW!' yelled Mira's big sister, Rani.

The only problem with Mira's excitement was that she was still strapped into the back seat of the car. And she had whacked Rani in the eye.

Dad turned around from the front as Mum parked the car in the leisure centre car park.

'Calm down, girls. You'll have a lovely time with your friends and unicorns, like always. Just try to make it there in one piece.'

Mira jiggled up and down in her seat. 'But Dad, it's going to be the Festival of Snow!'

Dad smiled. 'And what happens then?'

'I don't know! But it sounds like SNOW much fun!' said Mira.

Rani rolled her eyes at the joke, but Mira could tell her sister was super-excited about the festival too. They'd only had rubbishy rain-snow so far at home, but Mira didn't care, because snow at Unicorn School was extra magical. And there would be loads of it – Rani had told her that at last year's festival the snow came up to her elbows!

Also, they would be playing in the snow with their unicorns, which would make it even more magical (approximately seventy million times more magical, Mira estimated).

As they got out of the car they saw the queue of people by the bins, where the magical portal to Unicorn School was. Usually they were one of the first to arrive, because Mira and Rani would wake up at 5 a.m. and chant 'CAN WE LEAVE NOW?' at their parents until it wore them down. But today they'd been a bit delayed as Mira couldn't decide which snowsuit to pack (cats, pugs, pigs or watermelons). Eventually she packed all of them, plus a special snowsuit she'd made for her unicorn, Dave.

'I'm going to build the BIGGEST snowman at the festival,' said Rani, striding across the car park.

'I'm going to build the HUGEST

snowwoman,' said Mira. She was dragging her snowsuit-filled bag along the ground and had to run to keep up with her sister.

'Well, I'm going to build a snowdinosaur!' said Rani.

'I'm going to build a snowcat!' said Mira.

Rani scoffed. 'That's tiny compared to a snowdinosaur.'

'You didn't let me finish! I'm
going to build a snow-cat-robot-
giant-from-space.' Mira threw her
arms wide to show Rani just how big
it would be, but unfortunately managed to
whack Rani again, this time in the other eye.

Rani stomped off towards the bins and joined
the queue. There were only a couple of other
children left waiting to go through the portal
and Mira tried to drag her bag a bit faster – she
didn't want Dave to be waiting and wondering
where she was. (When Mira arrived at Unicorn
School, Dave was usually busy snacking, napping
or causing mischief – but maybe this time he'd be
waiting for her by the landing haystack?)

As Rani stepped into the bush behind the bins and went through the portal, Mira heard two familiar voices.

'Hey, Mira!'

Mira hugged the twins, Freya and Flo, from her class. They were late too!

'I've heard you can do snow-surfing at the Festival of Snow,' said Freya. 'It sounds awesome!'

'I want to try snow jumping!' said Flo.

'What's snow jumping?' said Mira.

'You jump in a load of snow!' said Flo.

'Amazing!' said Mira.

She was about to tell them about the snow-cat-robot-giant-from-space, when something bright orange appeared by her foot. It was a big neon boot

and it was attached to their friend Jake. He was standing on one leg and wiggling the boot at them.

'Ah! I see you're checking out my superpowered snow boots,' he said, changing legs and wiggling the other one. Then he stomped on the ground and lights flashed up and down the sides of the boots.

'Very cool!' said Freya.

'Actually, very warm,' said Jake. 'They're heated to melt snow and ice.'

'My snow boots have googly eyes,' said Flo.

Jake said that the snow activity he was most looking forward to was snow laser quest. 'Pegasus has been training for it,' he said.

'But we all know what the unicorns' favourite snow activity is . . .' said Freya.

'Making snow angels!' they all said together.

Unicorns LOVED rolling in the snow and making shapes. Although Mira knew that her unicorn would be more interested in the festival snacks.

Dave was a bit different to the other unicorns. While they were sparkly and glossy and pranced around very elegantly, Dave was grumpy and greedy and did giant poos in places where you weren't meant to do giant poos. Although he'd not been the unicorn Mira had expected when they first met, no one made her laugh as much as Dave! She loved her UBFF (Unicorn Best Friend Forever), and she couldn't wait for another adventure full of snacks and giant poos!

Soon it was Mira's turn to go through the magic portal. She dragged her bag into the bushes and reached for the special portal-opening flower. Mira gave the flower an extra-hard squeeze as she imagined the deep, sparkly snow that awaited her on the other side.

With a **WHOOOOOSH** Mira and her bag were sucked into the portal. She felt the familiar tingling in her chest as she hurtled along the rainbow. Stars and sparkles zoomed past her. This time Mira was sure she saw flurries of snow spiralling past as well!

Then the colours and flurries faded and Mira was falling through the air. She squeezed her eyes shut and landed with a **FLUMP** on the landing haystack.

Mira opened her eyes and looked around to see ...
NO. SNOW. WHATSOEVER.

ᑌᑌᑌ

'How can you have a Festival of Snow without

any snow?' said Mira's friend Darcy, who was

trotting along on her unicorn, Star, as they headed

through the paddock. Darcy and Star were both

covered in sparkly white fur: fake-fur-lined boots, hats, gloves and capes – even furry earmuffs and a horn-warmer for Star. They looked magnificent, but also a bit sweaty as it wasn't that cold.

'Do you think they'll rename it the Festival of No Snow?' said their friend Raheem, putting the matching bobble hats he'd brought for him and his unicorn, Brave, back in his bag.

But Mira had a much bigger question on her mind. How could you have Unicorn School without your UBFF? She couldn't see Dave anywhere!

Her unicorn was often off causing mischief when Mira arrived, but she'd usually found him by now. She'd checked all the usual places – the rainbowberry bush at the corner of the paddock, the canteen kitchen bins, his five secret snack hideouts – but there was no sign of her little grumpy unicorn. And now the teachers were calling them for assembly!

So . . . where was Dave?

CHAPTER TWO
No Snow Festival

'It's okay, Mira,' said Raheem, squeezing Mira's shoulder as they walked towards a big stage that had been set up in the paddock. 'Dave probably just got distracted during his third breakfast or his seventh nap. We'll track him down.'

The worried feeling in Mira's chest eased a bit. 'Thanks, Raheem!' she said, as they sat down with the rest of Class Red and their unicorns.

Assembly was outside because of the Festival of Snow. Everyone fidgeted in their hats and scarves and big coats as they realised they were actually quite warm. Mira left a Dave-sized space next to her.

'What do you think that is?' said Darcy,

pointing at the stage.

Behind the head teacher, Madame Shetland,

there was a glittering silver sheet draped over a

group of round lumps that looked like rugby balls,

but bigger. Surrounding the lumps were some

little bar radiators. Mira recognised those. Her

grandma Nani-ji had ones like them in her house.

But she had no idea what could be hiding under

the sheet!

'Maybe it's something to do with the festival?'

Mira said.

Their class teacher, Miss Glitterhorn, shushed

them and Madame Shetland began the assembly.

'I know everyone is looking forward to the Festival of Snow!' she said. 'And here's Dr Goodwhinny, who organises the festival each year, to give you a little update.'

Dr Goodwhinny was the geography teacher. 'I have something wonderful to show you!' she declared, as she stepped up onstage. Dr Goodwhinny's unicorn, Longshore-Drift, followed, dragging a tube-shaped machine covered with lots of little dials and screens. 'This is the Snow-o-Meter,' said Dr Goodwhinny proudly. 'It will track the snowfall at the Festival of Snow. It measures snow to the nearest nanometre and it goes up to two metres, which is the highest snow level ever recorded at Unicorn School!'

'What's it at now?' called out a girl from Class Green.

Dr Goodwhinny pressed a button and the machine started whirring and juddering. It gave a loud beep and she peered at one of the screens. 'Zero!' she said.

There were disappointed murmurs around the paddock. Then Madame Shetland, Dr Goodwhinny and some of the other teachers had a whispered conversation around the Snow-o-Meter.

Madame Shetland stepped forward. 'The Festival of Snow is postponed until tomorrow,' she said, 'while we wait for the snow.'

Dr Goodwhinny and Longshore-Drift dragged the Snow-o-Meter back offstage and the disappointed murmurs got louder.

Madame Shetland raised her hand. 'Never fear, children and unicorns – we have a few things to keep you occupied until then.' The paddock quietened down. 'The festival isn't the only special event we have this week. In two days we're having an Open Afternoon, for next term's new pupils to visit and see what Unicorn School is like, so I'd like you all to make them feel very welcome.'

'My little brother Calvin's coming!' said Jake. 'He's just like me but smaller. And less awesome, obviously.'

Mira thought the Open Afternoon sounded really fun. She had a brief daydream about the new kids following her around as she dispensed wise advice and told stories of her Unicorn

School adventures and they hung on her every word. And she couldn't believe there was going to be another Class Red – they wouldn't be the youngest ones any more!

Madame Shetland gestured to the mysterious lumps under the silver sheet. 'Finally,' she said,

'this is a little surprise for you all. And here's our special guest to unveil it!'

A woman ran onstage. She had wild grey hair and was wearing a dress made of leaves. Mira realised it was Ms Mustang, their old camping-trip instructor! Ms Mustang's unicorn, Wildebeest, suddenly appeared next to her. He was a trained survival unicorn and had camouflaged himself to blend in with the paddock fence.

'Afternoon, everyone!' said Ms Mustang.

'It's morning, Ms Mustang,' said Madame Shetland.

'Not for me – I get up at three a.m.,' said Ms Mustang. 'So, yesterday, I was out doing my daily powerjog, when I found these!'

She whipped off the silver sheet to reveal a clutch

of brightly coloured eggs nestling in a pile of straw.
They were a fiery orange colour and Mira thought
she could see bits of gold on them too.

'Can anyone tell me what they are?' said Ms
Mustang.

'I CAN!' Raheem shouted, loudly enough to
make Mira jump. He had his hand up in the air as
high as it would go.

'Yes, Raheem?' said Madame Shetland.

'I saw eggs just like that on a documentary,' said
Raheem. 'They're pocket fire-dragons!'

'Correct!' said Ms Mustang.

'Ooooooooh!' said everyone, and some of the
unicorns stomped their hooves.

'As luck would have it, there are seven eggs,' said

Madame Shetland. 'One for each class to look after.

And pocket fire-dragons are very good friends for

unicorns – they enjoy curling up in their manes.'

Mira couldn't believe it. Their own class pet!

And not just any pet, but an actual DRAGON.

'Dave, isn't that amazing!' she whispered, before

remembering that her UBFF was still hiding somewhere.

'Why's that egg at the back so massive?' said Darcy.

Behind the orange eggs sat a much bigger egg, covered in rainbows. Mira couldn't believe she hadn't noticed it.

'Oh, that's not a real egg,' said Madame Shetland. 'That's a decorative papier-mâché egg made by Miss Ponytail to celebrate. It's full of chocolates that we can share out later.'

Miss Ponytail, the art teacher, beamed and gave a little bow. 'Don't touch it, it's fragile!' she said.

A loud RUMBLE rang out from the stage, making everyone jump. It was coming from the egg

nest. Mira, Raheem and Darcy all looked at each other. Were they going to see a dragon hatch now?

The rumbling got louder and everyone leaned forward.

Mira saw something moving. But it wasn't the little orange eggs. It was the rainbow papier-mâché one.

The egg began to shake, and the rumbling got louder and louder.

Then there was a sharp **CRACK**, followed by a thundering **FART**. The top of the eggshell flew up into the air. And poking out of the egg was . . . not a dragon, but a unicorn's bum.

And not just any unicorn's bum . . .

'Dave!' yelled Mira.

CHAPTER THREE
The Wrong Crack

Mira's unicorn kicked his little legs and the rest of the rainbow papier-mâché eggshell shattered around him. Dave jumped down from the stage, trotted over and nuzzled his chocolate-covered face into Mira's neck.

'It's not Unicorn School until you turn up, Dave!' Mira said, giving her UBFF the biggest, squeeziest hug.

'He must have chewed his way inside to get to the chocolates,' Darcy said.

'He definitely found the cosiest spot for a nap,' said Raheem. 'Pocket fire-dragon eggs have to be kept really warm. That's why all the little radiators are there.'

'That reminds me!' said Mira. She rummaged through all the snowsuits in her bag, until she found the special snowsuit she'd made for Dave. It had a picture of a doughnut on the side and even a little bum flap at the back (which was necessary when your unicorn held the world record for the most poos in a minute).

'Though I guess it's not actually that cold today . . .' Mira said.

But Dave was already burrowing into the suit. Once inside, he let out a low, rumbling fart, blowing the bum flap open.

Miss Ponytail was sadly picking up shards of papier-mâché eggshell. Mira went over to help, followed by the rest of Class Red and their unicorns.

When they'd finished clearing up, Mira noticed something.

The nest was empty!

The rest of the school were huddled in their class groups, each admiring a shiny orange egg. Class Blue's egg had gold stripes. Class Green's had polka dots. Class Indigo's even had gold stars! Class Yellow were just getting down from the stage and Mira's sister, Rani, was clutching an egg with gold zigzags to her chest.

'They've given all the eggs out!' gasped Mira.

'WHAT!' said Darcy.

Darcy wheeled over to Madame Shetland. Class Red and their unicorns followed her. They all started up a chant of, '**WHAT DO WE WANT? OUR EGG! WHEN DO WE WANT IT? NOW!**'

'Of course, Class Red,' said Madame Shetland. 'Your egg is there.'

She pointed to the nest, where Dave was back having another nap.

At first Mira thought Madame Shetland was confused. But then . . .

Nestled next to Dave was another egg. It must have been hidden by the rainbow papier-mâché egg, so she hadn't noticed it before. It was a bit bigger than the other eggs, and the shell was bright white. Mira felt excited. They still had their very own pocket fire-dragon! Now they just had to wait for it to hatch . . .

∪∪∪

'I can't wait to see the dragon fly!' said Seb.

Back in their classroom, Class Red watched their egg. Each class had been given some of the straw and one of the little radiators, and they'd made their egg a new little nest in the reading corner.

'I'm going to stroke and hug our dragon so much!' said Tamsin.

'Dragons don't do hugs,' said Jake, shaking his head. 'I hope it hatches out of the egg breathing fire!'

'I hope it waits until we've got it out of the nest,' said Raheem, eyeing the straw.

'I'm going to film SO many dance videos with the dragon,' said Darcy.

'I'm going to tell it all my ideas for taking over the world,' said Flo.

Mira wondered what she was most looking forward to, but she couldn't decide. Everything about the dragon was going to be awesome! 'What are you looking forward to, Dave?' she asked.

Dave looked like he was thinking hard, but then Mira realised that it was his poo face. Sure enough, he unleashed a giant poo next to Pegasus's foot. Pegasus neighed crossly. As Mira shovelled it up with her poo shovel, she wondered what dragon poos were like.

They watched the egg and waited.

And they waited.

And they waited.

Then they waited some more.

Tamsin fidgeted and wriggled her legs. 'It's taking ages to hat–'

CRAAAAAAAAAAAAAAACK!

Class Red and their unicorns all sat bolt upright. Mira's heart thumped in her chest. She held her breath . . .

The egg didn't look any different.

CRAAAAAAAAAAAACK!

The sound was louder this time and was followed by cheers.

'That's coming from next door,' said Jake. 'It must be Class Yellow's egg.'

Sure enough, Rani came skipping through the door.

'Our egg hatched!' she said. 'It was amazing!

First it trembled and then sparkling cracks of light appeared all over it and then the CUTEST dragon with BIG, SPARKLY EYES poked its head out and chirped at us. We've called her Andromeda Butternut.' She skipped off again.

Class Red went back to watching their egg. They waited.

Soon there was another **CRACK** and cheering from the Class Orange classroom on Class Red's other side. It was quickly followed by more hatching sounds from down the corridor. Everyone was running into each other's classrooms and comparing hatching stories.

'Our dragon came out singing!' called Abeola from Class Orange.

'Ours has shimmering scales!' said Jimmy from Class Green.

Class Red's egg sat there. There was no trembling or singing or magical cracks of light.

'Come on, egg!' said Flo encouragingly, rustling the straw.

'Maybe it's not warm enough?' suggested Tamsin.

'I have a spare snowsuit!' said Mira, getting her sparkly purple one out of her bag. They popped the egg into it, and then added one of Raheem's bobble hats and Darcy's furry scarf. The egg looked very smart and cosy. But it still wasn't showing any signs of hatching. Then they tried heating it with Jake's ice-melting snow boots – still nothing.

'Is anyone a bit . . . bored?' said Seb.

The unicorns were getting restless.

'We should have taken them out for a prance
by now,' said Freya, looking at her unicorn,
Princess, who was pawing at the window with
her hooves.

Dave was eating a pile of textbooks out of desperation. It was way past the time he usually had his first lunch.

'I'm sure it will hatch soon, Dave,' said Mira, scratching him behind the ears.

Dave burped grumpily.

At least when their egg did hatch it was going to be super magical!

CHAPTER FOUR
Chilli-farts

The next morning Dr Goodwhinny's Snow-o-Meter was still showing zero, and the Festival of Snow was postponed for another day. It was replaced with Dragon Care lessons, so Ms Mustang joined the PE teacher, Miss Hind, for Dragon PE with the newly hatched dragons.

Everyone was super-excited – except for Class Red. They had fallen asleep in the reading corner, watching their egg all night, but their egg was very much still an egg.

All the other classes were out in the paddock with their dragons on leads. The dragons were a fiery red-orange colour with gold patterns, and were the size of rabbits, which made them more cute than fearsome.

Freya and Tamsin and their unicorns came out,
pushing Class Red's egg in a wheelbarrow.
It wouldn't have needed all of them, but Dave
had jumped into the wheelbarrow for a nap.

'Zeus is already flying,' Yusuf from Class Indigo was saying proudly.

'Oh, Andromeda Butternut skipped flying and went straight to soaring,' said Rani.

'Volcano breathed fire right after she was born,' said a boy from Class Violet. 'We had to get her out of the nest quickly so she didn't set the straw alight!'

Miss Hind blew her whistle and then began ticking off each dragon on the register. When she called Zeus's name, the little dragon flew a loop-the-loop and got a round of applause.

'Queen Funkleberry the Destroyer?' said Miss Hind.

'Yes!' cheered Class Blue, as their dragon puffed out some little fiery sparks.

'Dennis?'

'Yes!' chorused Class Green.

As Class Yellow all cheered for Andromeda Butternut, Mira and her friends looked at their egg. It didn't have a name!

'Mr Biscuit?' said Miss Hind.

'Yes!' sang Class Orange.

'And . . .?'

Class Red looked at their egg again.

'Egg?' said Mira.

Miss Hind wrote down the name and ticked it off.

The first part of the lesson was flying the dragons on their leads, while Class Red wheeled Egg around and Ms Mustang told them more about pocket fire-

dragons. Once they'd got their flying confidence, she said, they would be able to fly as high as the top turrets of the school. And they'd be breathing fire soon too, so oven gloves should be worn when handling them. Miss Hind handed round sets of gloves, along with bags of chilliberries, which Ms Mustang said were fire-dragons' favourite food. 'But they are very spicy for the rest of us!' she said.

Before Mira could stop him, Dave had stuck his nose into their bag of chilliberries and gobbled up a mouthful. He stopped. His face went red, his eyes went wide and watery, and he did a loud burp. Then he shrugged, stuck his nose back in the bag and ate some more.

A lovely warbling chirp rang out. Mira saw that

it had come from Zeus. Yusuf and the rest of Class Indigo looked at him in delight.

'Ah yes, you may notice your dragons starting to sing,' said Ms Mustang. 'Dragonsong is one of the most beautiful sounds in nature. Some even believe it has magical powers.'

Flo put her ear to Egg's shell. 'Nothing yet,' she said.

Mira couldn't wait to hear their dragon sing!

Miss Hind announced that they would finish the lesson with a flying race. The dragons were going to fly to the other end of the paddock and Miss Hind put down cones to mark the start and finish lines. Mira pushed Egg forward hopefully.

'Can Egg fly?' said Miss Hind, raising an eyebrow.

'Um, no, not yet,' said Mira, willing Egg to burst

out of its shell and swoop into the air.

'I'm afraid it will have to spectate then,' said Miss Hind.

'Aw, not fair!' said Jake.

Mira looked at all the little dragons limbering up and flapping their wings. Ms Mustang's unicorn, Wildebeest, was leading them in a warm-up of vigorous lunges. She felt sad for Egg.

'You'll be able to join in soon,' she said, giving Egg a pat. And then she had an idea. 'Can I commentate on the race, Miss Hind?' she said. 'That will help Egg feel more involved!' Back home Mira and Rani liked to commentate on their dad's cricket matches because it made them a lot less boring, even though he told them it really put him off his game.

44

'If you like,' said Miss Hind.

Mira popped Egg down next to her. Then she dragged Dave, with his mouth still in the chilliberry bag, to sit on her other side. 'You can be my co-commentator, Dave!' she said.

Dave snorted and chomped. He had his bum facing the race, but hopefully he could still contribute.

Mira grabbed a nearby twig to be her microphone. 'So, Dave, do you think we're in for a good race today?'

Dave burped.

'Yes, exactly,' said Mira. 'The dragons are raring to go. Zeus is flapping his wings and Andromeda Butternut is doing squats and –'

Miss Hind blew her whistle.

'– and they're off!' said Mira into her twig. 'Dennis has soared into an early lead, but Mr Biscuit has somersaulted past him and that's Zeus coming up the inside and WOW – Volcano is speeding through from the back and whatdoyouthink, Dave?'

Dave burped. He wiggled his bum behind Egg.

Mira took a breath. 'Queen Funkleberry the Destroyer is catching up and that's a lovely loop-the-loop from Andromeda Butternut but it's still Volcano, no it's Mr Biscuit, no it's Volcano, no . . .'

FRRRRRRRRRRRRRRRRRRRRRRRRP!

A thunderous fart erupted next to Mira and something whooshed past her. She shook her head and focused back on the race.

'It's Mr Biscuit, no it's Volcano, no it's Mr Biscuit, no it's . . .' A new shape had appeared in the sky, zooming to the front of the pack of dragons. Mira squinted up at it, then gasped, '. . . Egg!'

Egg was still an egg. But somehow it was soaring through the air above them – and winning the

race! Class Red leaped to their feet and cheered.

'Dave moved it with his fart!' said an awestruck Seb. 'The chilliberries must have given him some extra power.'

Mira thought she might burst with pride as Class Red quickly hopped on to their unicorns to get to the finish line before Egg landed.

'Egg is in the lead,' said Mira, continuing to commentate into her twig as she galloped along on Dave. She was throwing chilliberries ahead of them to make Dave go faster. 'Mr Biscuit is second, no Volcano, no Mr Biscuit – but will they catch Egg? No, they won't!'

'Egg wins,' called Miss Hind from the finish line.

Egg shot past Miss Hind's cones as the other dragons swooped back down. And then . . . Egg started to drop.

Mira quickly got the spare snowsuits out of her bag. Class Red laid them out on the ground underneath the falling egg. It landed in the pile of suits with a soft **WHUMP**.

Class Red danced a victory dance around Egg. The other classes were consoling their dragons when they were all hit with a **WHOOSH** of cold air. At first, Mira thought it might be the snow finally arriving – as if today could get any better! – but it was just the cookery teacher, Mr Nosebag, pushing a big freezer full of cold snacks.

'Don't we usually have hot snacks at the

Festival of Snow?' said Miss Hind.

But Mr Nosebag pointed out that it wasn't
the Festival of Snow yet, so he'd done something
a little different. 'Sherbet ice-blast slushies!' he
said. 'Maybe Dave could help me taste-test them
when they're ready?'

Dave threw his head back and gave a very
enthusiastic snort. Then he carried on munching
his chilliberries and let off another superpowered
chilli-fart, blasting Egg back up into the air.

Raheem ran and caught Egg before it flew
too high. He gave it a little hug – and then he
stopped. 'Oh my gosh – look!' he said.

All along one side of Egg's shell was a
shimmering blue crack.

CHAPTER FIVE
Chilly Fart-blasts

'Come on, Egg and Dave!' cheered Seb.

Class Red were back in their classroom and
Egg was back in its nest. Dave was in the nest too,
blasting Egg with more superpowered chilli-farts.
So far there was still just the one crack in the shell,
but they hoped a bit more fart-heat would do the
trick. Class Red took turns holding Egg (and their
noses) so it wasn't blasted out of the nest.

'Go, Dave!'

Mira was cheering the loudest. She could still
feel the little glow in her chest from her UBFF

helping them win the race. And now he was helping Egg to hatch!

WHOOOOOOOOOOOOOOOOOOOOOOOSH!

A draft of cold air blew in from the door. It was Mr Nosebag again with his freezer. Tamsin threw a scarf over Egg to keep it warm.

'The sherbet ice-blast slushies are ready to taste-test!' said Mr Nosebag.

Dave shot out of the nest and across the room. Mr Nosebag held out a bucket filled with neon-blue slushy ice. Mira thought it looked like a nice treat for Dave. He could probably do with a little break from all the fart-blasting.

But then Mira had another thought.

Frozen food meant frozen farts!

'No, Dave! Don't drink the ice-blast slushies!'
she said.

But it was too late – the bucket was nearly
empty. Dave burped.

'And we're out of chilliberries!' said Tamsin.

They decided to try giving Egg another fart-blast

anyway, but Dave's fart blew through the nest like an icy wind.

'N-n-n-nooooo!' shivered Jake.

Class Red slumped in the reading corner with their heads in their hands as Dave continued to fill the nest with chilling gusts.

'Shall we point him out of the window?' said Darcy.

Mira felt a lump in her throat. Dave was trying his best. It wasn't his fault dragons needed to be hot to hatch!

'W-w-w-wait – g-g-guys!' said Raheem, who was holding Egg and shivering.

Mira gasped. More cracks had appeared on Egg's shell!

CRAAAAAAAAAAAAAAAACK!

'Keep going, Dave!' cheered Flo, as Class Red jumped to their feet.

Dave released another icy blow-off. The shimmering cracks continued to spread. Then the egg began to tremble. Then it began to shake.

CRAAAAAA AAAAAACK!

The top of the eggshell flew off and landed on Pegasus's horn.

A blue head with big eyes and scales and two sharp little horns popped out of the egg. The dragon looked around at them all.

'Egg!' cheered Class Red.

Egg let out a very happy – and very loud –

'RAAAAAAAAAAAAAAAAAAAAAAAAAAAAAAAARRK!'

He jumped up and down, cracking the rest of his shell. Then he screamed again.

It wasn't quite magical singing, thought Mira. Maybe that came later. And it was nice that the dragon was so happy to see them!

'Hi, Egg!' she said, waving. 'I'm Mira.'

Egg screamed at her and clapped his claws.

They all introduced themselves and their unicorns and Egg screamed happily at each of them in turn. Then he spun around in a circle – his blue scaly tail whipping around the nest and knocking over the radiator.

'Is it weird that he's blue and all the other dragons are fiery red?' said Darcy.

'The hottest kind of fire is blue,' said Jake.

It wasn't just that Egg was blue. Where the other dragons had gold patterns, he had silver markings that looked a bit like stars. He was also bigger – about the size of a wastepaper bin. He was a bit different to the other dragons, but Mira liked it!

Egg did a big stretch, unfurled his bright turquoise wings and gave them a flap.

'I think he's going to fly!' said Freya.

Mira held her breath. Now this was going to be magical!

Egg started running very fast while flapping both his wings and his arms. He did a lap of the classroom and Class Red watched in delight, waiting for him to take off. Egg wiggled his tail

and flapped his wings again. Then he started skipping. He skipped twice around the classroom before turning to them all, looking very pleased with himself, and bowing.

'Well done, Egg!' yelled Flo, clapping enthusiastically. Everyone else joined in.

'He's just building up to flying,' said Jake confidently. 'Can you breathe fire, Egg?'

Egg blinked at him, and then took a big breath in.

'Quick, move the nest!' said Raheem.

Class Red rushed over and started pushing the straw away from the little blue dragon.

Egg blew out a puff of air.

'Here we go!' said Jake.

Egg blew out two more puffs of air. Then he

bowed again. Flo led another round of applause.

'His breath is freezing!' said Raheem.

'Maybe he just takes a while to warm up,' said Freya.

Then Tamsin stepped forward with Moonbeam, her unicorn, standing shyly behind her. 'Please may we stroke you, Egg?' Tamsin asked.

Egg bounded over, jumped up and wrapped his wings around her.

'Ooh, that's a very chilly hug!' said Tamsin. 'Th-th-th-thank you, Eg-g-g-g!'

Egg jumped up and hugged Moonbeam next. When he let go, some of her mane had frozen.

From the nest, Dave snored. He was taking a well-deserved nap now he'd hatched Egg. The dragon's head snapped around. Then he

bounded over and jumped on Dave.

Mira's eyes widened in alarm. Dave was

at his grumpiest when he was woken from

a nap! But Dave just looked at Egg and then

settled back down to sleep. He was very snug in

his snowsuit after all, so maybe he didn't mind

having a cold dragon sitting on him.

Mira looked at her UBFF and their new dragon friend. Unicorn School had just got even more fun!

∪∪∪

It was time for the next Dragon Care lesson, so Class Red headed out to the paddock where Ms Mustang and Wildebeest were waiting, surrounded by several big red warning signs.

The other classes were arriving with their dragons all nestled cutely between their unicorns' ears. Egg had wrapped himself around one of Dave's back legs and didn't seem to want to travel any other way. He was still absolutely freezing. Mira and her friends kept trying to warm him up by offering him hats and scarves, but he just kept wriggling out of them.

They reached the others. Mira managed to peel Egg off Dave, but he just attached himself to her instead. A chill rattled through her body. She patted Egg's cold head and he screamed happily at her, causing a couple of nearby unicorns to bolt.

Now they were closer, Mira could see that Ms Mustang's warning signs said:

DANGER –
FIRE!

'By now your dragons should have started to produce more fire,' said Ms Mustang, 'so make sure you have your oven gloves.' Wildebeest was poised nearby with a fire extinguisher. 'We'll start off easy – heating up some snacks!'

Miss Glitterhorn handed out toasting sticks and bags of marshmallows.

'They'll taste nicer toasted, Dave!' said Mira, whipping the bag out of reach of her unicorn, who had immediately made a lunge for it.

They went around the circle, each dragon having a go at toasting the marshmallows. Most were just making little flames like candles, but a couple shot out jets of fire that made everyone jump back.

When it was Egg's turn, Darcy held the toasting stick out. Class Red gathered around, encouraging him. Egg blew three puffs of cold air, and the marshmallow froze solid. Dave ate it.

Everyone else carried on toasting. But however hard they tried, Class Red could not coax any fire out of Egg. Ms Mustang came and showed them a technique of tickling the dragon's feet, which

was supposed to help. Egg just rolled around on his back letting out a high-pitched giggle, until they stopped tickling him. Then he froze another three marshmallows.

At lunchtime Egg clung to Dave again and froze more food, which the greedy little unicorn gobbled up. Mira's UBFF had clearly developed a taste for frozen food. He had frozen pizza, frozen chips and

three frozen doughnuts. Egg ate chilliberries, like the other dragons, but only after he'd frozen them.

After lunch, Class Red had Science. Egg was meant to light their Bunsen burner, but instead he froze all the contents of the test tubes and everything in the science cupboard. In Music they had to create a performance based around dragonsong, but Egg froze all the instruments and did some powerful scream-singing until the music teacher asked them to stop.

When they'd finished dinner, and Egg had frozen Dave's spaghetti bolognaise, it was time to put their dragon to bed. Class Red had removed the nest from the reading corner and replaced it with a bed made from scarves, blankets and one of Mira's snowsuits. But every time they put Egg in it, he sprang back out and wrapped himself around Dave's leg. Eventually they agreed that Egg could sleep in Dave's stable.

But even after they'd carried Egg's bed to the stable, he still wouldn't sleep in it. Instead, he climbed into Dave's snack mini-fridge.

'I guess he prefers a cold bed?' said Seb.

Once Dave had checked that Egg wasn't eating his snacks, he curled up in Egg's cosy bed himself. Egg jumped back out of the fridge to give them all one more chilly hug, and they said goodnight.

Although not what she'd expected, Mira was sure that 1) Egg was the friendliest dragon EVER, and 2) he was full of surprises!

CHAPTER SIX
Growing Pains

Egg had another surprise waiting for Class Red when they went to collect him and Dave from the stable the next morning.

'Oh my gosh!' said Darcy, as she wheeled through the stable door.

Dave's snack fridge was bulging. The dragon leaped out when he heard them arrive – he'd doubled in size! He was bigger than Dave now.

'We're meant to paint him sitting in a papier-mâché egg in Art!' said Freya. 'He won't fit in the one we made now.'

'Maybe he can just wear it as a hat?' said Mira, as Egg greeted them all with a chilly morning hug.

Before Art they had an emergency assembly where Madame Shetland told them that the Festival of Snow would be postponed again until the next day. 'However!' she said, raising her voice

above the disappointed groans. 'This allows us
to make a very special addition to the festival –
a performance by the pocket fire-dragons!'

The groans were replaced by ooooohs.

'What kind of performance?' asked Sarah from
Class Blue.

'It's up to you!' said Madame Shetland. 'But it
will be a lovely chance for the dragons to show
off their flying and fire-breathing skills. And
it's always a pleasure to hear some dragonsong.
So get together at lunchtime for your first
rehearsal.'

Class Red looked at each other and then at
Egg, who was lying on his back next to Dave
while they both snored loudly.

Mira wished Madame Shetland had included skipping, blowing cold puffs of air and screaming in her list of dragon skills. Would Egg be able to join in the performance?

∪∪∪

When Class Red got to the art room to do their painting of Egg, they put the papier-mâché egg they'd made on his head. It instantly froze and shattered into lots of pieces.

Mira saw Miss Ponytail coming over and was worried they would get into trouble, but Miss Ponytail just picked up one of the frozen eggshell pieces and held it up to the light.

'How lovely,' she said. 'A snowflake shape, like his markings!'

Mira looked at Egg in surprise. She'd thought his silver markings were stars, but Miss Ponytail was right – they were snowflakes!

Unfortunately, while they were talking, Egg had shattered all the other papier-mâché eggs that the rest of the classes had made for their dragon portraits, so Miss Ponytail had no choice but to give him three Havoc Points, which meant a lunchtime detention.

In a separate incident, Dave had eaten all the paintbrushes, so he had a detention too.

Mira and her friends dropped Egg and Dave off in one of the history classrooms, with Mr Trotsky there to look after them, and went off for lunch.

∪∪∪

The first rehearsal for the fire-dragon performance went ahead without Egg, and Mira watched as Dennis and Queen Funkleberry the Destroyer did a complicated set of figure of eights and somersaults, while Volcano drew a fiery heart in the air. She hoped Egg would be able to catch up.

But what Mira saw when she went to pick him up from detention blew all thoughts of the festival performance from her mind.

He'd grown again!

Egg now towered over Dave. In fact, he was bigger than most of the other unicorns. The rest of the fire-dragons weren't growing this fast. They didn't seem to have grown at all, really.

What was going on?

'Guys,' said Raheem. 'Do you think Egg is a different type of dragon to the others? He's nothing like the other pocket fire-dragons.'

The others nodded. 'Yeah, maybe he's like an ice dragon or something,' said Darcy.

'WHAT?!' came a shout from the corridor. Ms Mustang came running into the classroom, followed by Madame Shetland and their unicorns.

'Did someone say ice dragon?' said Ms Mustang, looking alarmed.

'Yes, that's what we think Egg is,' said Seb.

Ms Mustang looked up at the big blue dragon. Egg waved at her.

'I think you may be right,' she said grimly.

'Now nobody panic, and follow me.' Ms Mustang began walking slowly back towards the door. Wildebeest did the same.

'What are you doing?' said Darcy.

'*I'm staying very calm so I don't anger him,*'

Ms Mustang hissed out the side of her mouth.

'Egg's never angry!' said Tamsin.

'Ice dragons are extremely dangerous,' said Ms Mustang.

Mira laughed. 'That can't be true –'

She looked back at Egg and then forgot what she had been going to say. In the time they'd been talking, Egg had grown AGAIN! He waved enthusiastically at Mira and hit his head on the ceiling.

'And they grow to be enormous,' Ms Mustang continued. 'He should be in his natural habitat – the Icy Tundra.'

Mira gasped. She'd seen the Icy Tundra on a map once in one of their geography lessons – it was right in the very corner, which meant it must

be miles away. 'Egg won't be able to visit us from there!' she said.

The other dragons were going to be released to roam where they liked around the Unicorn School grounds and the Fearsome Forest, but they would come back to the school for food and to sleep.

Ms Mustang stepped forward carefully. Egg flipped on to his back with his legs in the air so she could tickle his tummy. The force of him hitting the ground made the whole room shake.

Ms Mustang pointed at him. 'A dangerous dragon like this cannot be a class pet!'

Egg's ears drooped. And if Mira's ears could droop, she knew they would have done too. Dave burped angrily. All of Class Red were distraught.

'Egg isn't dangerous – he's super friendly!' said Freya.

'Egg loves hugs!' said Tamsin.

'And he loves US!' said Jake.

Madame Shetland sighed. 'I'm sorry, Class Red, but Egg will need to be taken back to the Icy Tundra as soon as possible.'

The silence hung in the air, punctuated only by a mournful fart from Dave.

Mira swallowed. 'Can we at least take him to the Festival of Snow before he goes?' she said.

Madame Shetland considered this. 'Fine,' she said. 'We can take him tomorrow afternoon, so he can see some of the festival. But it's probably best he doesn't perform with the other dragons.

We don't want them getting scared.'

As the two teachers began discussing the arrangements for transporting Egg to the Icy Tundra, Mira looked around at her friends. They needed to think of a way to keep Egg!

CHAPTER SEVEN
Good Egg

'Maybe we can sneak in and break Egg out?' said Freya. It was after dinner, and Class Red were in Mira's dorm room having an emergency How-to-Save-Egg meeting.

Seb shook his head. 'We won't get past the teachers.'

Egg was still in the history classroom, with the teachers taking turns to keep an eye on him. Dave had wanted to stay with Egg and had to be dragged from the room. He made his feelings clear by doing a large protest poo in the corridor.

'Maybe we could put a hat and glasses on Egg as a disguise,' suggested Flo. 'And if anyone asks, we can just say he's a very tall man?'

But the rest of Class Red didn't think anyone would believe Egg was a very tall man.

Mira chewed on her fist, which she always did when she was thinking hard. How could they persuade Madame Shetland to let Egg stay? Her thoughts were interrupted by whoops, cheers and dragonsong drifting in from down the corridor. It must be another rehearsal for the Festival of Snow.

'If only he was allowed to join in the dragon show,' said Raheem, 'then the teachers would see how Not Scary he is!'

Maybe that was it!

'Madame Shetland only said he couldn't perform with the other dragons,' Mira said. 'So maybe Egg could do his own performance! And that would show everyone what a great pet he is!'

'I like it!' said Darcy, and Star clapped her hooves.

Mira got out her ideas notebook and they started to make a list of things Egg could do in his one-dragon show.

'He's good at knocking things over,' said Seb.

'And making them cold,' added Jake.

'Don't forget skipping!' said Flo.

'And hugs!' said Tamsin.

There was a pause. It wasn't sounding like a performance just yet.

'He could chill some food?' said Darcy.

Mira chewed her pen. She looked over at her unicorn. What would Dave do? Right now, what Dave was doing was putting some finishing touches to another protest poo.

Mira had a thought. 'Rani showed me a video on YouTube of someone teaching their cat to use the human toilet!'

'That's nice, Mira,' said Darcy.

'What I mean is, what if we could teach Egg some skills?' said Mira. 'Like you teach dogs to fetch and the way we taught all the unicorns, except Dave, to hop.'

'Would we be teaching Egg to use the human toilet?' said Tamsin, looking confused.

'No, that was just an example,' said Mira. 'We could teach him pet skills, like fetch, and something performance-y, like dancing!'

'I taught my hamster, Cookie, to dance!' said Seb.

'Let's do it!' said Darcy.

Class Red and their unicorns got to the history classroom just as Miss Hind and Miss Glitterhorn were taking over for the night shift, watching Egg. The teachers agreed that they could have half an hour with their dragon.

'Will that be enough time?' whispered Tamsin.

Mira was about to reply when Egg bounded over to her and licked her face with his

now-massive tongue. The force of it caused her to trip and fall into a nearby bin.

'It will have to be' said Jake, throwing a ball in the air. 'Come on, Egg!' Jake showed him the ball, then threw it across the room and pointed. 'Fetch!' he said.

Egg looked at the ball, then at Jake. Then he went and gave Jake a chilly hug. Jake threw the ball again, and Egg hugged him again. He tried ten more times, and got ten more chilly hugs.

'This isn't going well,' he said, turning on the

heat setting on his boots to warm himself up.
'I'll have one more go.'

Jake threw the ball, but this time Pegasus
trotted after it and picked it up in his mouth.

'No, Pegasus – Egg's meant to do it!' said Jake.

But when Pegasus dropped the ball, Egg ran
over and picked it up. Then they both ran back to
Jake, and Egg dropped the ball at his feet.

Class Red burst into applause.

'Good Egg!' yelled Flo.

They all took turns to pat Egg's cold head. The dragon looked delighted and jumped up and down, knocking over six desks. They did it again and again, with a different unicorn helping each time, and each time Egg followed the unicorn and fetched the ball. When it was Dave's turn, Dave tried to eat the ball and then sat on it, so Egg did the same.

'He loves copying the unicorns!' said Tamsin.

'Um, guys,' interrupted Jake. He showed them the time on his snow boots. The half an hour was up and they'd only done one trick!

'I think it's okay,' said Darcy, pointing over to the corner where the teachers were sitting. Miss

Glitterhorn was asleep with her head in her book, and Miss Hind was snoring. Miss Hind slept with one eye open, which was quite unnerving.

'Okay, guys,' Mira whispered. 'It's Egg time!'

UUU

In the next morning's assembly, Class Red and their unicorns couldn't stop yawning. They had been up all night training Egg, and had crept out in the morning when the teachers started to stir.

The training had gone well. Once they realised that Egg would copy everything the unicorns did, he had learned every trick they'd taught him. But Mira was still worried. Was it enough to show everyone that Egg was a good Egg?

In assembly, Dr Goodwhinny was giving a Snow-o-Meter update. 'It says two centimetres!' she said.

Mira took deep breaths. She had been wishing for snow, but now it was here she felt nervous — because it meant the Festival of Snow would go ahead, and that meant Egg's performance would be happening soon! The jittery feeling in her tummy even felt a bit like little flurries of snow.

She looked out of the window — but she couldn't see any snow.

'Oh, actually that's just a bit of porridge from my breakfast,' said Dr Goodwhinny, peering more closely at the Snow-o-Meter. 'The real snow level is . . . zero.'

Madame Shetland announced that the Festival of Snow was postponed until the next day.

Class Red all looked at each other. Mira panicked. Madame Shetland had said that Egg would be going back to the Icy Tundra that afternoon. It meant he wouldn't get to do his show!

Up on stage, the head teacher was looking at her watch. 'We don't have anything planned for the rest of assembly as we really thought the festival would be happening,' she said. 'Does anyone have something they'd like to share?'

Mira's hand shot straight up in the air. 'We do!'

∪∪∪

After Mira had told Madame Shetland that she could think of at least seventy-seven reasons why Egg performing would be a really good idea –

and not, in the words of Miss Hind, a disaster waiting to happen – and after Mira had begun listing the seventy-seven reasons, the head teacher had wearily agreed. So Class Red leaped up from their seats and ran to get Egg.

Mira led him up onstage, followed by the rest of Class Red and their unicorns. There were some gasps as the rest of the school hadn't seen Egg since he'd grown so big.

'We present the Magnificent Egg!' declared Mira.

Egg skipped forward, with the Class Red unicorns trotting either side of him – except for Dave, who was sitting snugly on the dragon's head. Egg's skips made the stage shake, and the crowd shrank back.

Mira raised her hand. 'Egg – stay!'

Egg and the unicorns stopped.

'Egg – sit!' said Jake.

The unicorns all sat down. Egg sat too.

The impact of him hitting the stage made the

unicorns bounce into the air, like a bouncy castle.

Next they did fetch, and then roll over. They went through all the tricks they'd taught Egg, the unicorns by his side the whole time, and the rest of the school started to clap and cheer in appreciation.

Darcy, who had planted herself in the audience, yelled, 'Wow – he's such a GOOD CLASS PET!'

'Who wants an ice lolly?' said Raheem, holding up a tray of lolly moulds filled with liquid. Lots of hands went up in the air.

'But those aren't frozen!' said Flo dramatically. 'WHAT WILL WE DO?'

'Egg – freeze!' said Seb.

Egg blew cold puffs of air over the trays and the lollies froze. Raheem handed them out to

cheers and whoops. Then Egg froze more lollies until everyone had one.

'I could use him in my kitchen!' said Mr Nosebag.

'I think he's actually THE BEST DRAGON EVER?' yelled Darcy.

The others in the crowd started chanting Egg's name. Mira chanted along and clenched her fists happily – it was going perfectly!

Then it was time for the grand finale – the dance. Darcy and Star had choreographed a totally epic routine that incorporated Egg's skipping, the unicorns' prancing and Dave's trademark bum wiggle. Everyone clapped along and some people were even copying the moves.

Then Mira saw a small shape scurrying on to the stage. It was one of the pocket fire-dragons. The little dragon dashed over to Egg, who was lying on his back and kicking his legs in the air while Dave bum-wiggled on his head. Mira saw the dragon tickle Egg's foot with its tail. Egg threw back his head.

'Nooooo!' said Mira, realising what was going to happen.

'RAAAAAAAAAAAAAAAAAAAAAAAAAAAAAAARRK!'

Egg let out what Class Red knew was his normal laugh, but to everyone else it sounded like a bloodcurdling shriek. Now he was bigger, the sound was deeper and more like a roar – it filled the whole hall.

The pocket dragon leaped up in the air, terrified, and Egg accidentally caught it with his foot as he kept on kicking his legs. The dragon flew back to Class Green, making scared (and very tuneful) whimpering sounds.

'Egg hurt Dennis!' said a girl called Tanya, stroking the fire-dragon protectively.

Up on stage, Egg kept roaring. More of the pocket dragons started to fly around in a frenzy. Some of the unicorns got spooked too.

'He's just laughing!' said Mira, but no one could hear her over the chaos.

'Everybody freeze!' said Madame Shetland. Egg looked at Madame Shetland with a confused expression, and then breathed out a big, cold blast

of air in the direction of the crowd. The dragons squealed, the children jumped back and the unicorns reared up and neighed.

Egg was in a real fluster now. He turned to Mira and the rest of Class Red, looking panicked. His tail whipped around and knocked all the teachers off their chairs.

'Enough!' thundered Madame Shetland.

Silence descended on the hall, apart from the harmonious chorus of whimpering pocket fire-dragons. Mira looked tentatively up at the head teacher, whose hair was completely frozen.

'That dragon has to go!' said Madame Shetland.

CHAPTER EIGHT
Let It Go

Mira's head bumped against the window of the snow bus. Normally she'd be so excited to be going on a Unicorn School trip – especially to a part of the land she'd never seen before. But the closer they got to the Icy Tundra, the sooner they'd be saying goodbye to Egg. It was so unfair!

Egg was being pulled along in a trailer behind them. His chin was resting on the edge of the trailer and his ears drooped. Dave was in the trailer too, and they were sipping on straws from an ice-blast slushie that Mr Nosebag had given them for the journey.

The bus jolted and bumped. It had special chains on the wheels for going through the snow – not that there was any snow yet. They jolted and bumped through the Fearsome Forest, then they jolted and bumped around the Crystal Mountains. Mira saw the village of Saddlebumstead off in the distance, and then it disappeared again. They were really going far! Soon she could feel a chill in the air.

Mira felt another jolt and opened her eyes to see Darcy tapping her on the shoulder. She must have fallen asleep! All of Class Red had their faces to the windows. Outside the bus, and everywhere that Mira could see, was dazzling white snow.

She twisted around to look at Egg. His ears had

pricked up and he was hanging off the edge of the
trailer with his tongue out.

The bus stopped and they all climbed off, their
shoes crunching on the crisp white powder. As an
icy wind whipped around them, Jake turned on
the heat setting on his boots. Mira was glad she was
wearing two snowsuits.

Egg bounded out of the trailer. He flipped on
to his back and rolled around happily, sending up
snow showers.

'See, Mira?' Madame Shetland said kindly. 'Egg
needs the snow and ice. And we don't have any of
that at Unicorn School.'

'All right, don't rub it in,' said Dr Goodwhinny,
who had come along to take photos of the landscape.

Mira nodded as she wiped the snow spray from her eyes. She could see how much Egg loved the snow. If only the Icy Tundra wasn't so far away!

Madame Shetland said they could play with Egg for a bit before heading back, so Class Red crunched their way over to Egg and tickled his tummy. The unicorns ran around whinnying and making snow angels. Then they all had a snowball fight – although whenever they threw snowballs at Egg, he would fetch them and bring them back.

'Good Egg!' said Mira, patting him and swallowing down the lump in her throat.

Dave spent the whole time wrapped around Egg's neck, a bit like how Egg had clung to Dave's leg when he'd first hatched. Mira's UBFF

looked like he was having the best time, especially as they kept stopping for ice-blast breaks.

But all too soon, Madame Shetland called for them to get back on the bus. It was time to say goodbye.

Egg looked around at them all with a confused expression and Mira knew he was wondering why they had all stopped playing. Class Red looked at each other. No one wanted to be the first to say it.

'TOO SAD!' yelled Flo, throwing herself face down in the snow.

Mira felt the lump rise back up in her throat.

'I'll do it,' said Jake. 'Egg . . .' Then he swallowed. '. . . I can't!'

Raheem stepped forward and took a deep breath. 'We have to go now, Egg,' he said. 'Thank you for

110

being the best class pet ever. I – I hope –' His voice cracked. 'I hope we can come back and see you sometime.'

Egg's ears drooped. Darcy and Star took a 'sadface' selfie. And Tamsin started to cry, loudly and snottily.

THUNK. Something fell next to Mira and made a small hole in the snow. **THUNK**. There was another. And another. Soon they were coming down like rain. Mira looked up and realised – Egg was crying frozen tears.

Class Red surrounded Egg and he gave each of them one last chilly hug. Mira shivered as she clung on to the dragon's freezing belly and he wrapped his wings around her.

'Goodbye, Egg,' she said.

III

Egg hugged them all again. Then he started a third round of hugs, but Madame Shetland said they had to hurry up. It took four people plus Mira to remove Dave from Egg's neck.

The dragon sat down in the snow with a thump and watched them get on to the bus.

They pulled away and Mira waved until Egg
was just a speck on the horizon.

UUU

When they got back, the unicorns went to their
stables for a rest and Class Red sat glumly in their
classroom.

Madame Shetland called an assembly at the end
of the day and Class Red and their unicorns sat
there with their heads down. Mira was surprised
to notice, however, that Dave seemed in quite a
chirpy mood. She had thought he would be the
saddest of them all. But he was sitting next to her
wiggling his bum and doing merry, tuneful burps
that were so loud Miss Glitterhorn shushed him.

Up on stage, Madame Shetland was explaining that Class Red had made the very difficult and mature decision to release their dragon into the Icy Tundra. 'And so I'm sure that another class will be happy to share their pet with Class Red.'

She picked Class Yellow.

Rani immediately tried to protest. 'Andromeda Butternut is very sensitive!'

Madame Shetland reminded her that it was kind to share, and then threatened her with a Havoc Point, and Rani reluctantly backed down.

'Hello!' said Tamsin, approaching Class Yellow's little fire-dragon. 'Would you like a hug?'

Andromeda Butternut hissed loudly.

Madame Shetland had another announcement.

'The Festival of Snow will be going ahead tomorrow,' she said. 'With or without snow.'

Cheers went up all around Class Red.

'The pocket fire-dragon performance is going to be epic!' said Yusuf.

Now they had the fire-dragon show, the other classes didn't seem bothered about the snow activities they would miss out on.

'Without snow, snow jumping is just jumping,' said Seb grumpily.

'This also means that the festival will run into our Open Afternoon,' said Madame Shetland. 'We had planned for our new recruits to experience a normal school day, but perhaps it will be nice for them to see what a Unicorn School party is like!'

Mira was still looking forward to showing the new pupils around. She'd even made a list of 'Top 20 Tips for Unicorn School' in her notebook. But it was such a shame she wouldn't be able to introduce them to the best class pet ever.

Class Red were still feeling sad all through dinner, but Dave was still strangely cheerful. He hummed little tunes to himself as he ate and then he trotted along tooting little joyful farts as Mira took him to his stable to go to bed. Then he dashed through the stable door and kicked it shut behind him and a few seconds later Mira could hear him snoring.

Mira frowned to herself as she walked back to her dorm. What was Dave up to?

CHAPTER NINE
Bum Snow

The next morning Rani got everyone up super early for one last practice of the fire-dragon performance. The teachers were all still in bed and the unicorns were asleep in their stables too, so they didn't have to come to the rehearsal.

Mira and the rest of Class Red arrived in the Great Hall. Rani was sitting in a chair with a sign saying 'Director' on it and was clicking her fingers a lot while yelling instructions.

Class Red sat down next to the rest of Class Yellow as Rani was telling a girl from Class

Orange to get her a babyccino and a croissant.
They thought they would try to get to know
Andromeda Butternut better, seeing as she was
their shared class pet now. But after the dragon
spat at them all and then bit Freya, they decided
to get to know her from a distance.

Rani told the pocket fire-dragons to practise
their grand finale. This involved them flying in a
big circle like a Ferris wheel, while each dragon
spun around breathing out smaller circles of fire.
Mira had to admit that it was very impressive.

'Hmm,' said Rani. 'It's good – but is it epic?'

'I think it's epic!' said Sarah from Class Blue,
as Queen Funkleberry the Destroyer swooped
down and perched on her arm.

'I think we can go bigger,' said Rani, standing up. 'We need more space – let's go outside.' She clicked her fingers and signalled to a boy from Class Green to pick up her chair.

They all followed Rani outside, Class Red trudging at the back of the group.

'Remember when Egg won the dragon race before he was even a dragon?' said Jake, as they approached the paddock.

'I miss him,' said Seb with a sigh.

'I could swear I heard his scream earlier,' said Freya, 'but it must have been the echo of a memory.'

'I want a chilly hug,' said Tamsin.

'I could hug you in the freezer?' suggested Flo.

'It wouldn't be the same,' said Tamsin. 'But thank you for offering.'

Mira wanted one of Egg's hugs too. And she couldn't wait for Dave to wake up and join them. At least if he was still in his happy mood, that might help cheer her up.

As Rani strode along the path towards the paddock, Andromeda Butternut leaped off her shoulder and up into the air. Everyone took a step back as the dragon flew around in a circle, breathing out a jet of fire.

'That's brilliant, AB,' said Rani. 'But we need to get to the paddock first.'

The dragon flew off in the opposite direction.

'Andromeda Butternut – stay!' called Rani, but the dragon just carried on flying. Then all the pocket fire-dragons rose into the air and zoomed after Andromeda Butternut. Everyone called for them to come back, but the dragons ignored them.

'Some dragons are so badly behaved,' said Jake.

'You've got to blame the parents really,' said Darcy.

'They're heading for the stable yard!' called Sarah from Class Blue.

'I think they want to see the unicorns!' said Yusuf, as they all hurried after the dragons.

They reached the stable yard a few moments after the dragons, who were forming a big circle in the air. Each dragon started spinning around. They were performing the grand finale! Rani clicked her fingers frantically and the boy from Class Green put down her director's chair. She sat back to watch.

Mira looked up into the sky. The patterns the dragons were making with their fire did look beautiful, but it would have been even better if Egg was there, skipping around and freezing things.

Then Mira smelled something odd. Not Dave-farting-after-broccoli odd, but a smoky sort of smell.

'The straw!' said Raheem, pointing.

Sparks from the dragons' flames had landed on a hay bale and clouds of smoke were rising into the air.

Mira looked in horror at the stable yard as more sparks fell on to the straw. Soon there were orange flames licking at the bales.

'**FIRE**!' yelled Darcy and Jake together.

Panic spread as everyone realised what was happening. The flames were getting higher and

more and more smoke was billowing into the
air. Then there were frightened neighs
from the stable doors on the other side
of the hay bales. The unicorns were
trapped!

Mira's heart was hammering in her
chest as she thought of Dave, alone and
scared in his stable. She looked at her
friends and she knew they were all
thinking the same thing – they had
to get to their UBFFs. But how?

Class Violet had sprinted off to get help. Everyone else was trying to call out to the unicorns to calm them – when something interrupted them all.

'RAAAAAAAAAAAAAAAAAAAAAAAAAAAAAARRK!'

An ear-piercing scream-roar rang out and a large figure burst into the stable yard, skipping very fast.

'RAAAAAAAAAAAAAAAAAAAAAAAAAAAAARRK!'

'Is it a monster?' said Yusuf.

'Is it a very tall man?' said Sarah from Class Blue.

'No . . .' said Jake.

'It's Egg!' Class Red all said together.

And it wasn't just Egg.

'It's Egg and Dave!' said Mira, staring in astonishment.

Mira's UBFF sat on Egg's shoulders, bouncing around as the dragon continued to skip, shaking the ground with every step. Egg must have followed them back from the Icy Tundra and hidden in Dave's stable! Now Mira knew why her UBFF had been in such a happy mood.

Egg opened his mouth wide. Mira thought he was going to scream again, but instead out came a jet of something very cold and sparkly – snow! Egg breathed jets of it over the hay bales, extinguishing the fires in an instant. The straw shimmered, frozen solid into zigzag patterns.

Egg didn't stop there. He skipped all around the yard, covering everything and everyone with a thick layer of glittering snow. Up on Egg's back,

Dave turned around. The bum flap of his snowsuit flew open and he fired out a fountain of frozen poo.

Mira gasped – and breathed in crisp chilly air. Every inch of the stable yard glittered white. The stable doors were framed in ice, and some of them even had icicles hanging down. Everyone gawped, stunned to suddenly find themselves covered in snow and standing in a winter wonderland. The unicorns came rushing happily out and started making snow angels.

But Egg and Dave still weren't done. Egg skipped out of the yard and continued to breathe snow and ice over all the Unicorn School buildings and grounds. Dave's jet of frozen poo showed no signs of slowing either.

'It must have been all those ice-blast slushies and chilly snacks,' said Mira proudly.

Darcy dramatically shook the snow out of her hair and Raheem wiped snowflakes off his glasses. Jake made a big show of switching on the heat setting on his boots.

Soon the school looked like an ice palace, with the turrets

shimmering silver in the winter sun. The paddock was covered in a thick layer of snow too. There was a loud BANG as Dr Goodwhinny's Snow-o-Meter exploded.

'Now THAT is epic,' said Rani.

'It's magical!' said Tamsin.

'What percentage of it do you think is bum snow?' said Darcy.

'Let's not think about that,' said Freya sensibly.

CHAPTER TEN
Unicorn School Forever

Eventually Egg and Dave finished their lap of the school and the dragon came skipping over to Class Red. Dave leaped off Egg's back and into Mira's arms. Mira squeezed her UBFF tight and ruffled his snowy mane.

Class Red surrounded Egg to make a fuss of him, but a voice interrupted them.

'It's a surprise to see you back, Egg,' said Madame Shetland. The rest of the teachers and

Ms Mustang were standing behind her.

Mira gulped. With all the magical snow-breathing, she hadn't seen the teachers arrive. Was Egg going to get in trouble for sneaking back to the school?

'But what a lucky surprise it is,' Madame Shetland continued. 'Your quick actions saved the unicorns and the whole school! And what's more, you've given us the snow we've all been waiting for!'

The stable yard erupted into applause and everyone chanted, 'Egg and Dave!' The unicorns clopped their hooves appreciatively. Rani clicked her fingers and told a girl from Class Orange to get Egg a frappuccino and an iced bun.

Madame Shetland said that Egg could stay. He had already turned Dave's stable into a mini Icy Tundra, so he could live there, and Dave was so cosy in his snowsuit that he wouldn't mind the cold. Dr Goodwhinny said it would be handy having Egg around, as then they could be sure of having snow for the festival each year, and Miss Glitterhorn said he could also keep an eye out in case the fire-dragons accidentally started more fires.

Then Madame Shetland presented Egg and
Dave with special Unicorn School Hero medals.
She even appointed Egg 'Outdoor Health and
Safety Monitor' because she said he was the most
well-behaved of all the class pets.

'I guess we just raised him right,' said Darcy, as
Class Violet's and Class Blue's dragons ran up
Mr Nosebag's trousers and bit his knees.

'That's because we did it as a team,' said Mira.
'And Class Red are the best team in the world.'

∪∪∪

The Festival of Snow was amazing. Darcy
took Egg snow-surfing and he screamed with
happiness so much that he needed a snow bath to

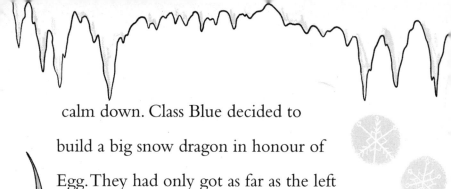

calm down. Class Blue decided to
build a big snow dragon in honour of
Egg. They had only got as far as the left

leg before they got tired, but everyone

agreed it was an excellent snow

dragon leg. They all had a brilliant

time snow jumping, except Jake,

whose special snow boots kept

melting the snow wherever he walked.

Then the pocket fire-dragons did
their performance, and Rani
had changed the ending so
the dragons fire-wrote Egg
in the air.

Even though it was cold now, the queue at
Mr Nosebag's ice-blast stall stretched
right across the paddock, and Dave
was alternating ice-blast slushies
with hot chocolates.

Then Tom 1 and
Tom 2 from Class
Orange came up and asked if
they could have a skipping ride on
Egg, which meant
that everyone wanted one
– and of course they all
wanted a chilly hug
at the end too.

In between snow activities, Class Red wandered around the stalls, though Mira ended up just following Dave to the ice-blast stall and then the hot-chocolate stall and back again. Dave was getting his seventh hot chocolate when Mira heard a burst of chatter from the entrance to the paddock.

'Welcome to Unicorn School!' Madame Shetland was saying, as she led in a group of children who were all younger than Mira and looked a mixture of super-excited and a bit nervous. Mira had forgotten about the Open Afternoon!

The children were all holding pieces of paper. When she got a bit closer, Mira saw that they'd drawn pictures of unicorns. She remembered drawing lots of pictures of her 'dream' unicorn before she met Dave. Her dream unicorn had been called Princess Delilah Sparklehoof and had been super-sparkly and elegant – and pretty much the opposite of Dave in every way.

Mira dragged Dave away from the drinks stalls and rushed over, eager to dazzle the new recruits with some wise words. She pulled her ideas notebook out of her bag. But when she reached them, the children were already chatting and marvelling at the unicorns. There was a boy taking selfies with Darcy and Star, and a girl was showing Raheem how the dream unicorn she'd drawn looked exactly like Brave. Lots of children were crowded around Jake and admiring Pegasus's golden mane and tail.

'I'm sure someone will come and admire you

soon, Dave,' said Mira.

Just then two girls started walking in their

direction. 'That unicorn looks AMAZING!' said one.

Mira grinned at them, but the girls walked

straight past and up to Freya and Princess. 'Please

can we plait her mane?' they asked together.

Mira sighed and sat down in the snow. Dave sat
down with a thump next to her. She supposed
that back when her dream unicorn was Princess
Delilah Sparklehoof, she might not have noticed
Dave either.

'Shall we make snow angels, Dave?' she said.

They lay on their backs, swooshing their arms

and legs in the snow, while Dave also did lots of
sherbet ice-blasty and hot chocolatey burps. Mira
looked up at the wintry blue sky.

'I'm so glad you're my UBFF,' she said, and
Dave farted loudly in agreement.

Then Egg skipped over, wanting to play with
Dave, and the two of them scampered around
chasing each other through the snow.

Mira sat up and saw a boy she hadn't seen
before, standing just apart from a group of new
kids who were taking turns to stroke Pegasus.
The boy wasn't talking to anyone and was
fiddling with his folded-up piece of paper.
He had scruffy blond hair and looked like a
small version of Jake.

'You must be Jake's brother!' she said.

The boy nodded. 'I'm Calvin,' he said, smiling shyly.

'I'm Mira,' she said, smiling back at him. 'I can tell you ALL about Unicorn School! Are you looking forward to it?'

'Yeah . . .' said Calvin, speaking quietly and shuffling his feet. 'It's just . . . my parents won, like, loads of medals when they were at Unicorn School and there's all these pictures of Jake and Pegasus on the fridge and all the amazing things they've done and . . . and what if I don't win any medals, or what if my unicorn doesn't like me or . . .'

Mira put a hand on Calvin's shoulder. Then she looked over at her UBFF, who was on Egg's back and doing a burping competition with him.

143

'When I first met my unicorn,' she said, 'he wasn't what I was expecting at all. But now I love him more than anything. And the things that make him different are the things that make him Dave.'

Calvin's eyes went wide. 'Is your unicorn Dave?'

Mira nodded.

'Jake's told me all about him,' said Calvin, unfolding his piece of paper. 'I'm his biggest fan!' He held the paper out to Mira. On it was a drawing of a small, grumpy-looking unicorn eating a doughnut with **DAVE IS THE BEST!** written above it.

Mira's heart soared and she went and got Dave to show him. Dave showed his appreciation by farting the alphabet and Calvin was delighted.

Then Dave started doing his bum-wiggle dance. Mira joined in and Calvin did too. Soon the rest of the new kids came over and started copying Dave's dance, agreeing that he was a pretty awesome unicorn.

'I can't believe you're bum-wiggling without me!' said Darcy, shimmying over with Star. Raheem and Brave bum-wiggled over next, followed by the rest of Class Red and Egg, who caused several mini avalanches as his tail swept from side to side.

Mira looked around at her best friends, and her Unicorn Best Friend Forever, as they all bum-wiggled their hearts out. Unicorn School had never felt more magical.

Rani, Angelica and Andromeda Butternut
bum-wiggled over next. Then Darcy tapped Mira
on the arm. 'Oh my gosh!' she said, pointing.
There were Miss Glitterhorn, Madame Shetland
and Miss Hind, all bum-wiggling away. Miss Hind
was particularly vigorous.

Calvin bum-wiggled through the crowd and
over to Mira. 'What were you going to tell me
about Unicorn School?' he asked.

Mira could tell that even though dancing
with Dave had made Calvin happy, he was
still a bit nervous. She looked down at her
notebook and the list of tips. And then she
put it back in her rucksack.

'Unicorn School will be full of surprises,' she said smiling. 'But you'll love it.'

Next to Mira, Dave nodded wisely. Then he unleashed a heap of frozen poo all over her feet.

Catch up on ALL of Mira and Dave's Adventures at Unicorn School!